"THE LINE UP"

By

Alley M

SCENE 1

EXT. THE PORCH OF STORM'S HOUSE - SUMMER
AFTERNOON

STORM, 27, Tall, slender, brown skinned and
KILLA, 26, average height, medium build, brown
skinned are sitting on the stoop when ACE, 25,
short, skinny, light skinned walks up to them
talking on the phone.

                    KILLA
          Yo

               ACE
               (Still on the phone,
          acknowledged both of them)
          Yo

               STORM
          What's good?

               ACE
               (To Asia on the
          phone)
          Yo I'm gonna call you
          back...

               (Kisses teeth)
          Yo I said I'll call you

back… ight

(Hangs up)

STORM

(To Ace)

Yo, you good?

ACE

That was Asia

KILLA

Yo… You still talk to her?

ACE

Yea... why?

KILLA

Na just asking

ACE

(Gives him a dirty look)

Niggas are funny...anyway

KILLA

Fuck you mean?

                    ACE

           (Ace inches closer to Killa)

Yo... I'm saying...

             ACE

What's good?

            STORM

Yo ya'll chill it's not even
that serious... word

             ACE

Fuck it... yo what y'all
niggas been up to?

            STORM

           (Storm looks at Killa)

You already know I'm tryna
get this wave...You wit' it?

(STORM LOOKS AT ACE)

            KILLA

Hell yea...you already know
that

                    ACE

     Na... I'm not even wit' that

(Both Killa and Storm stare at Ace)

                  STORM

     You got that bitch Asia
     making you soft? Since when
     you not with that?

                    ACE

     Watch your mouth son...
     Y'all don't get tired of
     doing the same shit all day
     every day? Sitting here only
     making us broke and shit
     getting hot out here too?
     I'm good

                  STORM

     Yo son, shit is legit, trust

                  KILLA

     Y'all niggas better start
     making some moves

                    ACE

     Y'all got it, I'm trying to
     get my G.E.D and shit…
     getting too old for the
     bullshit

                    KILLA

       This nigga washed up

              (Laughs)

       No bitch gonna stop my
       bread... word

(Storm laughs)

                    STORM

          You feel me Killa?

                    ACE

          Yo I'm 'bout to be out, what y'all
    niggas about to get into?

                    STORM

          My bitch supposed to be coming
       through

                    KILLA

          I'm tryna make some moves, 'bout to
       hit the block...

                    ACE

       Ight so I'mma check y'all later

                    STORM

          Ight

                    KILLA

Hood

Each person walks their separate way, down the
block where Ace is stopped by an unknown
female, MYSTERY, 26, average height, brown
skinned.

                    MYSTERY

        You Ace right?

                     ACE

        Who you?

                    MYSTERY

            (Smirks)

        No need for names, who your shortie?

                     ACE

        Yo why you asking me all these
    questions?

                    MYSTERY

            (Laughs)

        You answering them

She walks away slowly, Ace runs up to her,
turning her around by the shoulder.

                     ACE

        Yo... the fuck you doing...

MYSTERY

I ain't your bitch… watch how you talking to me

ACE

I'm saying though what's good with all the questions? And then you just gonna walk away… na son… you tryna deal with me or something?

MYSTERY

(Scoffs at him and walks away)

You?

ACE

(Shouting, arms raised in air)

YO SON WHAT THE FUCK

[Mystery walks out of sight]

SCENE 2

INT. ACE'S BEDROOM - AFTERNOON

Ace is on the phone with Storm.

ACE

Yea shortie tried to press me

    (Laughs)

Talking about who my shortie… yea

    (Laughs)

    Word… on some shit though… like am I Ace… fuck that   bitch though… you tryna link

He exits the bedroom and heads to the living room where he begins to straighten up.

INT. ACE'S LIVING ROOM – SAME DAY – 20 MINUTES LATER - CONTINOUS

Storm arrives

ASIA, 26, short, thick, light skinned arrives, she enters the living room where Storm and Ace are and she waves to Storm.

              STORM

    What up?

Asia sits down

              Ace

      (Addresses Asia)

What's good?

> Asia

Nothing...

> Ace

What you was fucking it?

> ASIA

Nothing, just wanted to get out of the house

> ACE

I hear that...

> (Addresses Storm rubbing his stomach as he speaks)

> Yo I ain't even gonna lie a nigga starving

Both Asia and Storm laugh.

> STORM

I feel you

> ACE

> (Addresses Asia)

What you got?

                    ACE

        I'm saying what you got? You got
bread or na?

                    ASIA

        I got enough… what y'all want to eat

                    ACE

            (Addresses Storm)

        Yo… you tryna fuck with I-Hop?

                    STORM

        Why not…

                    ACE

        Say no more

They all exit the house and head to I-Hop.

SCENE 3

INT. I-HOP – AFTERNOON

Asia, Ace and Storm sit at the table awaiting
their orders

                    ACE

     Yo, now that I think about it… I
think I've seen that bitch before

                  STORM

     Oh the one you were talking about
earlier?

                    ACE

Yea

                  STORM

Oh in the hood?

                    ACE

          (Laughs)

     Hell yea… that crazy bitch

Asia kisses her teeth loudly, Ace turns to
face her.

                    ACE

     Yo… you good?

                  ASIA

          (Mumbles)

Yea

Ace moves in closer to Asia leaning into her
face.

ACE

Yo… don't make me get out of character in here... you hear me?

ASIA

(Looks down at her plate and mumbles)

Yea…

ACE

(Raises his voice slightly)

No, do you hear me?

STORM

Yo chill son… chill

ACE

Na she starting that jealous shit again… anyway…

STORM

(Addresses Ace)

So… yo… you sure you not with this mission?

ACE

I don't know, I ain't really tryna fuck my shit up na mean shit getting to buck out here, they on it now… I just came home; niggas gotta see it from my side

                         STORM

     I hear all of that but this shit right
here… wavy… there go the bread for the G.E.D
right there

                         ACE

     We don't even need to be talking about
this shit in here

                         STORM

     So we out?

                         ACE

          (Ace looks to Asia)

     Yea

                         ACE

     We out

                         ASIA

     We gotta wait for the bill

                         ACE

     Fuck that shit…

Asia, Storm and Ace exit I-Hop
inconspicuously.

SCENE 4

INT. KILLA'S HOUSE - NIGHT

KILLA'S MOM, 40, has the looks of a hard life is on the couch smoking.

                    KILLA'S MOM

          Fuck you been?

                    KILLA

          Here we go again

                    KILLA'S MOM

          (Looks him up and down)
Humph, just like your piece of shit father

                    KILLA

          Yo… whatever…

                    KILLA'S MOM

          Yup and you can whatever your ass
right up on outta here… just like your daddy
both of ya'll ain't worth shit… you a hustla?

She gets off the couch and walks up to him purposefully snatching the money from his hand.

          You ain't no fucking hustla, a real
hustla would make sure home is straight first

                    KILLA

     So… basically you kicking me out?

She gives him an empty stare

                    KILLA

     Aight… say no more

SCENE 5

EXT - THE BUILDING - AFTERNOON

Ace and Storm are having a conversation when
Killa walks up.

                    KILLA

     What's good?

                    STORM

     We out here, what you fucking with?

Killa sits on stoop next to storm.

                    KILLA

     Son… shit got buck in the crib

                                              17

yesterday, real buck

                    STORM

        Oh word?

                    ACE

        Oh with moms?

                    KILLA

            (Looks at Ace)

        Son you already know

                    STORM

        What the fuck happened?

                    KILLA

        Son you know moms be wilding, she
kicked me out

                    ACE

        She kicked you out? For what?

                    STORM

        Na son...

                    KILLA

        Word to... she kicked me out *last
night* my nigga

                    ACE

        Last night?

                    KILLA

        Last night

STORM

That's crazy, yo you can stay at my
crib 'till your situation a little better
if you need to… for real… shit crazy

KILLA

Good looking my G

ACE

What happened though?

KILLA

I Couldn't even tell you, real talk,
just went up in there last night and it
was like she was dead ass waiting on me
just to come at me crazy… fuck it
though.. what's the word?

ACE

Ain't shit

STORM

(Addresses Ace)

Yo you ever found out who that bitch
was?

ACE

Fuck that bitch, only birds do that
type of suspect shit… and then Asia
bugging

STORM

I saw

ACE

This bitch always got a fucking
attitude, she know what time it is
already

STORM

(Laughs)

You know that's wifey don't even
front... you be tryna keep her away from
niggas so we don't see... surprised she
ain't pregnant yet

There is an awkward moment of silence when
Killa's phone rings.

KILLA

(To the person on the phone)

Yo... yea I'm still with it... you fucking
with it still? Oh ight hood...

(Hangs up)

Yo let me go handle this little mission real
quick

STORM

Definitely, get that bread

KILLA

Links

Killa walks down the block and turns the
corner where he sees Mystery in front of the
corner store, she is staring at him, he walks
up to her.

KILLA

Good afternoon beautiful

MYSTERY

(She licks her lips while looking up
and down) What up?

KILLA

What you doing just standing here on
this nice day?]

MYSTERY

Handling my shit…

KILLA

Yea… I can see that… grown woman
things

MYSTERY

You better believe it

KILLA

So I'm saying… what's good? You got
a number? Maybe we can talk some more
later… I got a few things I need to
handle myself…

MYSTERY

(She raises her eyebrow in
suspicion)

You asking for a number when I ain't
even get a name?

                    KILLA

          (Laughs and holds out his hand
for a hand shake)

          You right… my fault… Killa…

                  MYSTERY

          (In seductive voice)

     Oh… Killa…

She whispers in his ear her phone number he
takes it down in his phone.

                    KILLA

     (He backs up slowly and looks at her
sexually)

So… I'mma hit you up a little later, remember
that's Killa… *bedroom* Killa…

She smiles at him and nods his way, he returns
the gesture.

CUT TO:

EXT. - THE BUILDING - PRESENT TIME

Ace and Storm are still sitting in front of
the building talking.

                    ACE

That's crazy… how this nigga end up getting kicked out the crib?

 STORM

I don't know

ACE

He slipping, all he has to do is just go home… his moms is mad cool… why would he fuck that up? To be in the streets?

STORM

Always two sides to a story… you know how moms can get… they be riffing for no reason at all…

ACE

I don't give a fuck, my moms could bitch at me all she want at the end of the day she's the one that keeps that roof over my head… word…

STORM

I get where he coming from though

ACE

Fuck it though, he been moving funny lately anyway

STORM

How?

                    ACE

        He my nigga and all but that nigga a
jealous type nigga

                    STORM

        Killa? Na...

                    ACE

        That's my word he jealous of me...
just watch how that nigga move... you'll see
what I mean

                    STORM

        We making these moves though or
what? Time is money

                    ACE

        We out

They head for the bus stop.

SCENE 6

INT. ACE'S KITCHEN - EVENING

Asia and Ace are at the table.

                    ACE

          What you wanted to talk to me about?

                    ASIA

          Um… I… ugh…

                    ACE

              (Bangs on table with impatience)

          WHAT the fuck is it?

                    ASIA

              (Startled)

          I'm pregnant…

                    ACE

              (Gets up from table)

NA!... *na*... Come again? You what?

                    ASIA

        Pregnant

                    ACE

        BITCH! You better go get an
abortion!

                    ASIA

            (In a sarcastic tone)

        I'm three months already I can't get
one...

He mumbles under his breath and paces around
in a panic then leaves in a heated state
without Asia.

Scene 7

EXT - MANHATTAN - AFTERNOON

Ace, Killa and Storm are walking down the
street.

ACE

Why Asia tell me last night that
she's pregnant?

STORM

(Bends over in laughter)

Oh word... I jinxed you?

ACE

Hell yea, it ain't funny though

STORM

Shit, it is to me... so what you gonna
do?

ACE

Can't do shit now, she's three
months already, too late

KILLA

I don't know why you even getting
amped, you were dealing with it so... shit
happens... just make sure it's yours

ACE

It better be mines...

KILLA

You say it like you know...

ACE

(Beginning to become annoyed
with him he gives Killa a stern stare)

... I do know...

KILLA

(Laughs)

You sure about that?

ACE

Fuck is that suppose to mean? Yo...
I've been noticing you been on some funny
shit lately

KILLA

Not me... I just speak the truth]

(Laughs)

Real talk

Ace steps to his face.

                    ACE

        So what you wanna do then fam? You
over here talking all that slick shit… what
up?

                    KILLA

            (Scoffs)

        It ain't even that serious

                    ACE

        Don't move like a bitch!

Storm tries to step in between them.

                    STORM

        Fuck y'all niggas doing man…

                    ACE

        Stop moving like a BITCH!

                    KILLA

You pressing me over a bitch…

(His voice rises with exaggeration)

A bitch my nigga…

ACE

That *bitch* is carrying my seed… fall the fuck back! You gonna respect it or I'm gonna make you respect it!

Storm looks at the passer-byers who are staring at them.

STORM

YO! Y'all chill! Y'all making shit mad hot, this ain't the place for that we in the city. I'm not tryna get locked for nobody. Y'all niggas need to just chill.

Ace and Killa back away from each slowly and the three of them continue on their way.

Scene 8

INT. ACE'S KITCHEN – EVENING

Asia is sitting at the table when Ace walks

in.

                    ACE

        Yo is there something you want to
        tell me about you and Killa?

                    ASIA

        No...

                    ACE

           (Raises his eyebrow)
        You sure?

                    ASIA

        Yea...

                    ACE

        Ight...

                    ASIA

        Why?

                    ACE

              I just want to know why this nigga
         feel like he can talk crazy to me about
         you all the time

     Silence.

                         ACE

         Oh… so you ain't got nothing to say?

     Asia looks at him confused.

                         ASIA

         So what you want me to say?

     He moves in closer to her with a sly look on
     his face.

                         ACE

         Say you fucked him

                         ASIA

         I didn't

     He grabs her throat with force.

                    ACE
               (In a menacing whisper)
          Say it...

                    ASIA
               (Struggling to speak)
          I didn't

                    ACE
               (Raises his voice)
          Say it... say it...
               (Screams)...
          SAY IT!

Ace begins to choke Asia harder.

                    ASIA
          STOP! The baby!

Ace let go of Asia's throat and backed away
from her, grabbing his keys and heading to the
door.

                    ACE
          (Breathing heavy)

Good… and I want to make sure you never get the idea to neither

He leaves the house.

Scene 9

EXT. WINGATE PARK – MORNING

Killa and Mystery sit on the steps overlooking the track.

                    KIILA

          So… you gonna tell me your name
or na?

                    MYSTERY

          I'll tell you… only cause you
gonna help me with this little mission.

                    KILLA

          Mission? Ight… what's your name
though… what you go by?

MYSTERY

Mystery your misery.

KILLA

Oh word?

(Laughs)

I dig it... so what's this mission you got in mind?

MYSTERY

You cool with Ace right?

KILLA

Yea that's my nigga

MYSTERY

Not as of today

KILLA

What you mean?

MYSTERY

Not as of today you not, you gonna be on my side... you see that bitch Asia?

                    KILLA

        Yeah that's his girl… how you
know about her?

                    MYSTERY

        You see my peoples sent me to
handle her; you know how the game go… I know
all of you… by name…

                    KILLA

        So why you asked for my name?

                    MYSTERY

        Just playing the game… *just*
playing the game

                    KILLA

        Ma… you bugging… that's my
man's and his pregnant girl.

                    MYSTERY

        I don't give a fuck. This stays
between us by the way. We gonna do what we got
to do

        (In a seductive voice)

        And don't tell me no…

KILLA

Oh word? I like the way you move still you know, might fuck with you...

MYSTERY

Really? And to what do I owe this honor?

KILLA

That's my nigga... but on the other hand that's not *really* my nigga... you understand?

MYSTERY

Of course... I already told you he wasn't... I can see it *all* in your eyes

KILLA

I mean don't get shit twisted now... I ain't a snake... but... me, myself and I come first... I never forget what motherfuckers say to me

MYSTERY

So you with it? We ain't gotta
do nothing crazy, just teach him a lesson

                    (She smirks as she pats him
on his shoulder)

          You guys are *so* easy

                        KILLA

                (Looks around)

          Let's be out, I'm pretty sure you
have some things to do Ms. Mystery and so do I

They exit the park.

Scene 10

INT. SILK'S HOUSE - NIGHT

SILK, 27, brown skinned pretty boy and Mystery
are in the living room.

                        SILK

          Report?

                        MYSTERY

          Wasn't even hard, no challenge,

straight pimped him.

                    SILK

          You sure? Nigga might snitch

                 MYSTERY

          Silk I know how to play the
game... come on now... I learned from the best

                    SILK

          I hope you really did

          (Laughs)

          Females always swear they know
everything. Even *if* you learned from me... there
will only ever be one me... who can do it like
me? Now... how you so sure he wit' it?

                 MYSTERY

          Trust... dude feeling me I got
into that mental deep... he's wide open... he
don't really care about that nigga... that's how
dudes are... I ain't need *you* to teach me that...
I'm a female

                    SILK

          I hear you. What up about Asia?

                 MYSTERY

I heard she's pregnant?

Awkward silence.

                    SILK

          Oh word… off that shit too…

                    MYSTERY

          … *Na*... na… That's too much for
me… I'm not really trying to kill anyone let
alone a baby

                    SILK

               (Exaggerating his tone)

          So… the fuck you was planning on
doing then?

                    MYSTERY

          Kidnap them, fuck them up and
teach him a lesson

He laughs at Mystery as he gets up from where
he is and goes to the door motioning for
Mystery to come to where he is standing.

                    SILK

Just play the game ma

(He pushes her out the door and slams it behind her)

Just play the game

EXT. DOWNTOWN – AFTERNOON

Ace, Killa and Storm are walking on Fulton Street.

                    KILLA

               (To Ace)

          So you cool now?

                    ACE

               (He scowls at him)

          Some what...

                    STORM

               YO! Y'all niggas don't even start that shit today... word... I ain't with it; y'all beef every other day... shit getting old now.

                    KILLA

        Ace the nigga that's mad
sensitive… you know what they say… the truth
hurts

                    STORM

        Man, fuck all of that. Ace, you
missed *out* my nigga that mission was a great
look, could've had that bread

                    ACE

        Yeah? I dig it… I don't know if
I'm fucking with the school tings anymore

                    STORM

        Why not?

                    ACE

        Asia man… how I'm gonna get a
J-O? I need one asap, that school shit gonna
take too long

                    STORM

        Six months though? You gonna
knock that out in no time

                    ACE

          Yeah… but son, she's three
months right now my g, remember I didn't even
start that shit yet. Three plus six…

                    STORM

          Damn son and she might drop
before that

                    ACE

          Word

                    STORM

          So you ever seen that crazy
bitch again?]

                    ACE

               (Laughs)

          Yo you know we gonna be
laughing off of that forever… hood rats

               (Shakes his head)

          … Na not at all actually

                    STORM

          Where you had seen her at

though?

                    ACE

          Right around the corner, right
in front of Ahk

                    STORM

          Oh word?

                    ACE

          Yea… she stopped *me* my nigga
                (Laughs)
          … She never gave me her name
though

                    STORM

             (Notices Killa is zoned out)
          Yo… you good my g?

                    KILLA

          Huh? Oh yea, yea… just
remembered something I had to do… I'll link
y'all later.

He walks off down the street; Storm looks at
Ace with a confused look.

                    ACE

          I *told* you that nigga be acting
funny

                         STORM

               The fuck was all of that about…
that nigga bugged…

Ace and Storm shake their heads in disbelief
and keep smoking.

Scene 12

INT. ACE'S LIVING ROOM - EVENING

                    ASIA

          I have something to tell you

                    ACE

          You always got something to
tell me

                    ASIA
                (Stares at him)
            It's important…

Ace takes a seat.

                    ACE
            What...

                    ASIA
            I made a huge mistake…

                    ACE
            The fuck you mean you made a
mistake?

                    ASIA
            I don't… I don't think… I don't
know how to say this…

                    ACE
            Just keep it one hundred

                    ASIA

The baby isn't yours…

                    ACE

          Oh, so you a smut?

          (Laughs)

          I knew it… that's why I *asked*
you… so whose is it? Killa's?

                    ASIA

          Na…

Ace rises from where is sitting and moves in
closer to Asia.

                    ACE

          (He speaks methodically)

          Yo… *who* the fuck is that
baby's?

He puts his hand on Asia's stomach with force.

                    ASIA

          (Speaking out of breath,
almost in a pant while staring at him)

          No one

Ace squeezes her stomach a little harder as he
moves in closer to her face.

                    ACE

          Na... couldn't be *no* one's, don't
lie to me... you scared? You scared of me?

She nods yes, he pushes into her stomach with
great force.

                    ACE

          And you better be BITCH! Get
your sorry smut ass out my crib and go find
your baby daddy 'cause it ain't me BITCH!

She exits the house and he proceeds to blast
loudly on his stereo "Bitches ain't shit."

Scene 13

EXT. NOSTRAND AVE - MORNING

Ace and Storm are walking on the avenue.

                    ACE

          You'll never believe what the
fuck Asia told me yesterday

                    STORM

          What?

ACE

Son, this bitch told me that
the baby ain't mines

Storm looks at him as if he lost his mind.

STORM

Get the fuck out of here

ACE

Word to

STORM

Son, that's buck, the fuck you
do?]

ACE

God, I kicked that bitch out

STORM

Son I'm surprised you ain't
fuck her up

ACE

I'm almost did

STORM

After she already told you it
was yours, can't trust these females nigga,
not even my bitch I don't put nothing past
her, fuck that

ACE

Yo real talk, at the moment I
don't even want to talk about her ass no more
cause I *will* fuck her ass up

STORM

So what you trying to fuck
with?

ACE

Let's go get some bread, fuck
it

STORM

Ight

They exit the house and head down the street.

                    STORM

        So… son she ain't tell you who
it could be?

                    ACE

        Na…

Ace and Storm stop walking at the same time
and stare at each other.

                    ACE

        (Dismissive)

        Na…

                    STORM

        Yea my nigga, she already lied
to you about that being your seed. You said
Killa was acting funny…

                    ACE

        Na! Fuck that! I'll kill him

They continue walking until they stop in front
of a house

                    STORM

        I'm telling you

(Looks up over at the house)

Yo I wonder if Spragga in the crib

They walk up to the front door of the house. After ringing the bell several times SPRAGGA, 26, short, brown skinned finally comes to the door.

SPRAGGA

(Laughing)

What's good, what ya'll soft ass niggas doing on my block?

STORM

(Laughs)

Fuck out of here, you gonna let us in or we gonna have to bang?

He lets them into the house.

Scene 14

INT. KINGS PLAZA MALL - AFTERNOON

Ace, Storm and Spragga are walking through the mall looking at different women as they pass by, deciding which store to go into. Ace and Spragga agree on one store while Storm walks to a different one where he runs into Killa.

                    STORM

          Oh shit, what up nigga?

                    KILLA

          Chilling, what you dealing
with?

                    STORM

          Shit, here with Ace, I'm just
copping something light maybe some 'Lo you
already know how I do Speaking of… he told me
yesterday that seed ain't his.

                    KILLA

          Word?

                    STORM

          (Gives him a funny look)
          Yea… he ain't tell you?

                    KILLA

          Na, how he know that though?

                    STORM

          Son, she told him

                    KILLA

          That's crazy

                    STORM

               That's what I'm saying, like
     how the fuck? He be keeping that on *lock*

                    KILLA

               (Laughs)
               I don't really care though,
     ain't my bitch. The fuck you mean?

                    STORM

          Yo, that ain't your's right?

                    KILLA

          Hell na…

                    KILLA

          (Raises his voice)

          SON! The fuck are you talking

about?

                    STORM

        Son, you've been acting mad funny,
keep it real, I been peep the way you be
watching her anyway

Killa steps to Storm's face

                    KILLA

        Be careful nigga, be *very* careful,
you can't always trust friends

He bursts out into such a loud, evil laugh
that people walking past stare at him, after
realizing what he is doing he walks off. Storm
meets back up with Ace and Spragga, they
continue on walking to another store.

Scene 15

INT. STORM'S APARTMENT - EVENING - SAME DAY

Killa, Storm and Ace are smoking.

                    STORM

(Addresses Killa)

You done bugging my nigga?

KILLA

Fuck that shit

ACE

What y'all niggas talking
about?

KILLA

Your bitch… na fuck that, that
ain't your bitch, you don't know *who* bitch she
is

He chuckles to himself.

STORM

That's what I'm talking about,
you wild disrespectful my nigga.

ACE

I'm not even tight though, fuck
it, it is what it is

                    STORM

          This nigga started wilding when
I asked him about Asia

                    KILLA

          Niggas not suppose to be
calling out they mans over a next man bitch,
that's some real bitch made shit

                    ACE

               (To Storm)

          Asked him *what* about her?

               (Pauses)

          Yo, you told him?

                    STORM

               Yea nigga...

                    ACE

               (Shakes his head in
disbelief)

          Wow... niggas is wild. That's how
the fuck niggas moving now a days? Talk about
bitch made...

                    KILLA

            I wouldn't even have shit to
say if I ain't know about it, the fuck nigga
pressing me like that's my seed or something,
fuck outta here

                    STORM

            Yo, fuck you Killa, real ta

                    KILLA

            Na, I wouldn't say that if I
was you.

Killa puts down his L and begins to leave the
apartment facing them he slowly begins to
smile, laughing as he finally makes his exit.

Scene 16

EXT. WINGATE PARK — MORNING

                    MYSTERY

          So how we gonna do this?

                    KILLA

          When we doing this?

                    MYSTERY

              (Smirk)

          Tomorrow nigga

                    KILLA

          Shit you ready hugh? Ight

                    MYSTERY

              Hell yea, I'm thirsty for
some blood

                    KILLA

          You on that vamping shit?

                    (Laughs)

          I see you. Yo how we gonna
know where they are?

                    MYSTERY

          That's your call, Mr.
Killa

                    KILLA

                    (Laughs)

          I can dig it, he did tell
me he had to meet up with her tomorrow night
in the forties so I'll just call him a little
earlier see what he fucking with

                    MYSTERY

          Sounds delicious, now, I'm
gunning for that bitch Asia first, you gonna
be in the cut waiting. When you see him coming
at me you run up on him. Yo you see this…

Mystery pulls out a knife out of her pocket.

                    KILLA

                    (Laughs)

          That's light weight

Mystery gives Killa a 'come on' look.

                    KILLA

          It's cool though and keep
giving me that look I'll give you something
that's gonna keep you thirsty for real

                   MYSTERY

          Never mix business with
pleasure; you'll end up like Asia

Mystery puts the knife back in her pocket and
gets up from the bench walking away.

                    KILLA

          What you mean by that?

Mystery just keeps walking away ignoring
Killa.

Scene 17

EXT. EAST 42ND STREET - NIGHT

Asia is waiting for Ace on the corner when he
finally walks up.

ACE

What up?

ASIA

Nothing

ACE

Don't think we cool now
cause we not... you heard?

ASIA

Yeah...

ACE

Do you hear me?

ASIA

I *heard* you

ACE

Ight... and Storm is in the
crib, don't say shit to him I don't care what
that nigga ask you, you got me? Don't. say.
shit. to. him

                    ASIA

              Yeah...

                    ACE

                    Yo... if I catch you... yo
just remember what I said

They head down the street.

                    ASIA

              (Kisses teeth)

         I *got it*... damn

Ace stopped walking and stared at her as she
put her head down.

                    ACE

                    That's what I thought;
calm your little hot ass down

As they continue Mystery appears from nowhere
and runs up on Asia wearing a mask, knife
pulled out.

                    ASIA

                          ACE!

                          ACE

                   What the fuck!

                        MYSTERY

                       (To Asia)

                   SHUT THE FUCK UP AND WALK
BITCH!

Ace runs up into Mystery's face squaring up
when Killa runs up to Ace knife drawn with a
mask on.

                          ACE

                   YO! What the fuck!

                         KILLA

                   SHUT THE FUCK UP! JUST
KEEP WALKING AND DON'T MAKE A SCENE!

Killa placed his arm around Ace's neck and
Mystery did the same with Asia. The four of
them walk to a car that is waiting for them.
Silk is sitting in the driver's seat. Silk
drives to Ace's house, there he makes them get
out in a hurry before anyone could spot them.
Storm is in the house asleep. They head

upstairs, tying Ace and Asia up to the chairs
in the kitchen.

                         ASIA

               Silk?

                    SILK

          What up? How's my baby?

                    ACE

               (To Asia)

          His baby? Yo... you know him?
That's his seed? Yo, you set me up!

                  MYSTERY

          (Removing her mask)

     I wouldn't put it past her...

                    ACE

     Yo! Ain't you that bitch!

                  MYSTERY

               Oh no, no, no, don't do
that... no need for name calling... looks like
you're the bitch right now

Storm awakes and heads out into the kitchen.

                   STORM

                    WHAT THE FUCK... MYSTERY?
THE FUCK YOU DOING!

                         ACE

          Son, you know her too?
That's the crazy bitch I've been telling you
about!

                         STORM

          This my girl

  Killa removes his mask Storm, Ace and Asia
are shocked.

          ACE   STORM
ASIA

                    Killa?

                         KILLA

          Ight y'all niggas done?
'Cause I'm ready to do this. Asia, I love you
but you know how this shit goes, you owe the
man

Ace looks at Asia with an eyebrow raised.

                         ASIA

Dealing with you was a mistake Silk

                    SILK

                  (Laughs)

          That baby wasn't a mistake though now was it? Any way fuck all the small talk, won't be much talking going down soon anyway

Silk nods to Killa who hands him the knife he had in his hand. Silk walks over to Asia, yanking her head back by her hair running the knife along her throat and down to the middle of her chest then to her stomach, driving the knife in.

                    SILK

              I giveth and I taketh

                    ACE

          YO! Fuck that! STORM! NIGGA YOU JUST GONNA STAND THERE!

Storm stands in shock as Killa stabs him as well.

                  MYSTERY

          (Shakes his head and looks at Storm on the floor)

>   *Ain't that some shit, oh*
> *well.*

Mystery looks to Silk.

>   SILK
>   (Look at Killa)
>   Well nigga finish what you
> started…

>   KILLA
>   What *I* started?

>   SILK
>   (Looks at him sternly)
>   What *you* started...

Meanwhile Ace is able to get out of the tie,
he jumps out of the chair, runs over to Silk
grabbing the knife and they wrestle for the
knife until Ace is able to get it. Killa backs
away from them.

                    ACE

          NA! Where the fuck y'all
going?

Killa and Silk start to back away from Ace.
Mystery walks over to where Ace is standing.

                    ACE

          Motherfuckers stabbed my
girl, the homie, it ain't going down like
that! Somebody gonna pay!

                  MYSTERY

          Ace…

She places her hand on his shoulder.

                    ACE

          FUCK OFF ME BITCH!

                  MYSTERY

          None of them loyal Ace…
          (Whispers in his ear)
          None of them…

                              SILK

                    Yo, you turning on me?

                            MYSTERY

                    Just playing the game,
          just playing the game

Mystery helps Asia up from a crouching
position and lies her flat on back on the
floor.

                              ACE

                    I'm gonna let y'all decide
but motherfuckers got a hot five minutes to
get the fuck up outta here!

Killa and Silk walk to the door.

                             SILK

                    Yo Mystery! Get your ass
over here!

Mystery continues to stand by Ace.

                             SILK

                    Ight bitch!

                    KILLA

                    (To Ace as he exits the
house)

                    This ain't over my nigga

Silk follows behind Killa. Mystery helps Storm
up from the floor. Ace calls 911 and they wait
for the ambulance to arrive.

          FADE OUT:

                    The End

www.ingramcontent.com/pod-product-compliance
Lightning Source LLC
Chambersburg PA
CBHW060135260626
47160CB00005B/2112